For bee-friendly readers everywhere.

D1493851

C 03 0302123

ISBN: 978-1-913339-06-7
Text copyright - Helen Mortimer 2021
Illustrations copyright - Katie Cottle 2021

OMAR, THE BEES AND ME

By Helen Mortimer & Katie Cottle

First published in the UK
2021 by Owlet Press
www.owletpress.com

Bees feed from flowers. It's called foraging.

They love the sugary liquid called nectar.

We can make 'bee corridors' by planting flowers for bees and other insects to feed on.

There would be no fruit or seeds for us to eat without bees!

It all started when Omar brought a small slice of his mum's special honey cake for show and tell.

Omar was new in our class.

'My grandpa used to keep bees,' he said, quietly.
'He had apricot trees and jasmine bushes in his
sunny garden, a long way away.'

It gave Mr Ellory-Jones a fun idea. (He always has lots of fun ideas.)

We made apricot blossom out of pink tissue -
all scrunched up - and cut white
paper stars for jasmine flowers.

It was the first time I saw Omar smile.

Then we stuck them up and down the corridor outside our classroom. 'It's a bee corridor now!' laughed Mr Ellory-Jones.

We pretended to be like little bees, buzzing from flower to flower. I smiled at Omar. 'My grandad keeps bees, too,' I whispered.

Mr Ellory-Jones told us all about how
important bees are and that we should make our world
more bee friendly by growing flowers for them to feed on.

'But where are the bees?' asked Kurt.

'And the flowers?' said Nish.

'Sometimes it is only
the queen bee that
stays alive over winter,'
said Mr Ellory-Jones.

'And some bees hibernate.
But there will be bees again
in the spring, when it's warm enough
for the flowers to come out.'

At playtime I sat by the bins in the corner of the playground, watching the lorries on the road and the noisy building site. Everything was grey.

It gave ME (my name's Maisie by the way) an idea!

'We should make a REAL bee corridor!' I said. 'All the way from our school to the park next to my grandad's garden. He's got a beehive!'

Mr Ellory-Jones agreed it was a great idea.
The next day we chose some wildflower seeds (the kinds that bees love).
Sylvie helped Mr Ellory-Jones to fill out the order.

We shook them into envelopes and wrote out the instructions:
'Please plant these seeds in a pot and put them on your windowsill.
Water them when the soil is getting dry. Thank you from Class One.'

The next day we delivered the envelopes
to everyone in town, from our school
all the way to the park.

We did a lot of walking,
but some grown-ups came to
help out and Mr Ellory-Jones'
husband brought snacks.

Mr Ellory-Jones explained
that it would take some time
for the flowers to grow.
At least until next year.

It seemed like such a long time to wait. Every day we wondered how our seeds were doing. Mr Ellory-Jones kept us busy with stuff. Omar and me got the BEST parts in the Christmas show.

We were both bees!

Then in the spring, the magic started.

Every day, when me and Omar walked home together,
we saw more and more green spikes in tubs on the windowsills.

Soon the spikes sprouted some leaves.

Things didn't look so grey.

Then it was summer
and suddenly there were . . .

. . . wild flowers!

There were poppies and
cornflowers and foxgloves -
all the way from our
school to the park.

By the time the holidays came
me and Omar were best friends.

My dad called us 'Momar'
which he said was short for
'Maisie and Omar' because
we did everything together.

Most days we went to the park and then helped Grandad in his garden. All his flowers seemed to fizz while the bees buzzed in and out of them. 'I just can't believe how many bees there are this year,' said Grandad.

'That's because of Omar,' I said. 'And Mr Ellory-Jones.'

'And the bee corridor,' said Omar
and we both started to buzz like bees,
which made Grandad laugh.

TODAY:

SHOW AND TELL

We've got a different teacher this year - Mrs Chopra.
But we still do show and tell. I brought in a jar of
honey from my grandad's bees.

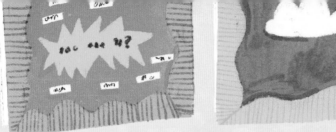

'This jar happened because we made a bee corridor
and the bees made the honey,' I said.
'And it's for Omar to say thank you for being my friend.'

Omar smiled the biggest smile I've ever seen.

And the next day . . .

. . . there was a WHOLE honey cake
from Omar's mum for all the class to share.

Bees are found all over the world. There are more than 20,000 different types of bees! Like Omar's grandpa and Maisie's grandad, there are beekeepers in every country.

Honey Cake Recipe

Ingredients

250g plain flour
4 eggs
150g sugar
100g runny honey
250g butter, softened
1 tsp baking powder
A pinch of salt

Method

Beat the butter until it is creamy and then add the sugar.

Add the honey, salt, baking powder, flour and eggs,
mixing well after each ingredient.

With the help of a grown up, pour the mixture into
a greased and lined cake tin and then let them put it
in the oven at 160 degrees (fan assisted)
for 45 minutes, or until it's golden.

Follow @owletpress on social media
or visit www.owletpress.com to learn more about us.